MR. GREEDY
and the Gingerbread Man

Roger Hargreaves

Original concept by
Roger Hargreaves

Written and illustrated by
Adam Hargreaves

EGMONT

D1355280

It was not long after he'd finished his breakfast that Mr Greedy started to feel hungry again.

He had eaten three packets of cornflakes, two loaves of bread and one pot of jam, but Mr Greedy's tummy was telling him that it was feeling peckish.

"What to have?" thought Mr Greedy to himself.

"I know," he said out loud.

"I shall make a gingerbread man."

And because he is Mr Greedy, he made an extra large gingerbread man, which he put in the oven.

And while he was waiting for it to bake, he had a snack.

A chocolate biscuit.

Followed by two more chocolate biscuits.

In fact a whole packet of chocolate biscuits.

And as he finished the last biscuit, he heard a knocking sound.

It was coming from the oven.

"How odd," he thought to himself and he opened the oven door.

And to his great surprise, out jumped his gingerbread man who ran round the kitchen crying:

"Run, run as fast as you can!
You can't catch me, I'm the Gingerbread Man!"

The Gingerbread Man ran out of the door and down the garden path.

Mr Greedy gave chase, but the Gingerbread Man was right. Mr Greedy couldn't catch him, and the Gingerbread Man was soon out of sight.

The Gingerbread Man ran up a hill and at the top he passed Mr Bump fetching water from a well.

"Run, run as fast as you can!
You can't catch me, I'm the Gingerbread Man!"

Mr Bump gave chase, but …

Oops!

Mr Bump tripped over his pail of water and rolled all the way down the hill and bumped his head.

The Gingerbread Man ran on.

He ran past Mr Lazy, asleep in his hammock.

"Run, run as fast as you can!
You can't catch me, I'm the Gingerbread Man!"

Mr Lazy opened an eye.

"You're not wrong," he said and he went back
to sleep.

On ran the Gingerbread Man.

He ran past Little Miss Late.

"Run, run as fast as you can!
You can't catch me, I'm the Gingerbread Man!"

Little Miss Late took up the chase, but the
Gingerbread Man was too fast.

"Oh dear. I can't even catch a bus, let alone
the Gingerbread Man," sighed Little Miss Late.

Nobody could catch the Gingerbread Man.

Mr Slow was too slow.

Mr Muddle got in a muddle and ran the wrong way.

Even Mr Tickle's extraordinarily long arms were not long enough to catch the Gingerbread Man.

"Nobody can catch me," boasted the Gingerbread Man, and he was so pleased with himself that he decided to lie down for a rest.

And he fell fast asleep.

"Caught you," said a voice, and a big pink hand picked up the Gingerbread Man.

"Slow and steady wins the race," continued Mr Greedy.

Mr Greedy took a big bite of the Gingerbread Man.

"Oh dear!" cried the Gingerbread Man. "I'm a quarter gone!"

Mr Greedy took another bite.

"Oh dear! Now I'm half gone!"

And another bite.

"Oh dear! I'm three quarters gone!"

And then one last bite.

"Oh dear," said Mr Greedy. "Now it's all gone …"

"… and I'm still hungry!"